CONTENTS

The Hangover

Dead Man Drinking

The Hangover

✝

1

Her skin smelled of flowers...

The party was in full swing when Curtis first noticed the girl. She was on the far side of the room, but she didn't seem to be with anyone. She shot him a dazzling smile and began to push her way through the crowd towards him. She had long black hair and dark hazel eyes. She was the most beautiful girl Curtis had ever seen, and now she was standing right in front of him!

The roar of the music pounding out of the sound system shook the floor. Curtis felt the girl's warm breath on his cheek as she put her face close to his. Her skin smelled of flowers.

"I can't hear myself think in here!" she shouted at him. "Let's go somewhere quieter!"

Without waiting for a reply, she took Curtis's hand and led him through the kitchen and out into the back garden.

Even outside the thud of the music vibrated the air. The girl gave Curtis a quick flash of her dark eyes. "I'm Pilar," she said.

"I'm Curtis."

It was dark in the garden. Nobody took much notice of Curtis and Pilar. Nobody saw Curtis drinking steadily from a bottle of wine that had been left on the decking, and certainly, nobody saw them leave.

~2~

Nice place you've got...

They got out of the taxi and Pilar paid the driver. Curtis looked around as the first leaves of autumn swirled down the street. He wasn't quite sure what part of the town they were in. In the taxi, he'd had his eyes on Pilar too much to notice where they were heading. And to be honest, he felt just a little bit drunk. Well, perhaps more than just a little bit...

Pilar stepped up to a large pair of doors, tapped in a security code and ushered Curtis into the apartment building. She pressed the button for the lift, which came almost immediately.

Inside the flat, Curtis sank down into a
large soft sofa. "I'll get us a drink," Pilar said,
and kicking off her shoes, she headed into
the kitchen.

The blinds on the large windows weren't down. Curtis could see hundreds of city lights fuzzy and indistinct in the haze of the city.

Pilar placed two glasses on the coffee table in front of the sofa. "There you go," she said.

"Thanks," said Curtis. "Nice place you've got here."

"It's not exactly mine," said Pilar. "I couldn't afford a flat like this on my own. I share it with a couple of girlfriends. They're away for the weekend," she added, flashing Curtis a quick smile. Curtis smiled back.

While Pilar went to the far side of the room to turn down the lights, Curtis took a sip of his drink. Then he watched her as she set some soulful music playing. Curtis took another, longer sip of his drink.

By the time Pilar came and sat down on the sofa next to him, his glass was empty. Curtis felt the warmth of her body up close against him.

But when he tried to look at Pilar, her face began to dance in and out of focus. When he looked away, the room started to spin.

3

This was no nightmare...

Slowly, Curtis became aware of a pain in his side; as intense and piercing as a scream. His whole body ached. He shivered. He was cold. And wet. He opened his eyes and could just make out row upon row of corrugated iron fencing reaching up to a grey, early morning sky. Somewhere, not far off, he could hear a dog barking angrily.

Curtis put out his hand and felt the rough, hard texture of a cinder track, and then something wet, like a puddle. Was he in a nightmare? He closed his eyes again, desperate to wake up. Then he opened his eyes slowly and the reality hit him like a train. The cinder track he was lying on was real; the cold and wet was real; and above all, the pain was real.

This was no nightmare. This was his morning.

He had been drugged and then beaten up. But why? Instinctively, Curtis put his hand towards his trouser pocket to check for his phone and wallet. As his hand passed over the constant, stabbing ache down his side, he noticed his fingers become damp and sticky. With an effort he raised his hand up and saw that it was stained with blood. When he put his hand down onto the cinder track where the puddle was, he realised that was blood, too. His blood. He'd been not just beaten up, but knifed as well.

He tried once again to shout, but his voice had become silent, trapped somehow inside his body. He tried to move, but the pain in his side was too great.

With a deep and agonised groan, he drifted back into the darkness.

—4—

Everything shook and swayed...

When Curtis opened his eyes again, the nightmare had changed. The corrugated iron fence and grey early-morning sky had been replaced by a piercing light angled right down into the depths of his eyes. A monster with a green body and white hands and bulging bug-like eyes peered down into his face.

"Curtis! Curtis! Stay with us," the monster was saying.

Suddenly, everything shook and swayed first one way and then the other. Curtis struggled, trying to free himself, trying to get away from the green, bug-eyed monster.

"Whoa, calm down," said the monster.
"We'll soon be at the hospital."

When Curtis opened his eyes the next time, the bug-eyed monster and the shining light were gone. But the pain in his side was still there, even if it didn't feel quite as sharp.

His eyes took in his new surroundings. He was on a bed in a white, clinical, windowless room. Everywhere, monitors and machines bleeped away.

The door opened and a man in a white coat came in.

"I'm Dr Hussein," he said. "You're a very lucky young man, Curtis. You must be a strong lad to have survived what you've been through."

Curtis didn't feel lucky or particularly strong. He felt confused. What had he been through? What was going on?

As if reading his mind, the doctor said: "You have quite a severe knife wound."

Curtis shook his head slowly. "I don't remember being attacked," he mumbled.

"You wouldn't," Dr Hussein replied. "You were drugged first."

"But why?" asked Curtis, weakly. "I don't get it. What did they steal?"

"Well, they didn't take your phone or your wallet," said Dr Hussein. "That's how the paramedics found out your name. But, yes, it was robbery."

Curtis tried to make sense of what Dr Hussein was saying, but he couldn't.

"What you must understand, Curtis, is that you weren't stabbed in some sort of street knife attack. No, you were attacked with skill and precision. The knife used to cut you open –"

Curtis flinched.

"– was one of these." Dr Hussein reached out and picked up a scalpel from a trolley by Curtis's bed. "A surgeon's knife." He twisted the handle round between his forefinger and thumb, and watched it reflect the white hospital lights.

"But if they didn't take my mobile or my wallet, what did they take?" asked Curtis.

Dr Hussein looked down at the large dressing to the side of Curtis's stomach, just below his ribs. "They took one of your kidneys. Your left one to be precise. Not a particularly complicated procedure for any half-competent surgeon to perform, but potentially fatal, nonetheless."

Curtis gagged. His stomach cramped up. He wanted to be sick, but the pain that shot up through his body stopped him retching. He couldn't believe what he had just heard. He didn't want to believe what he had just heard. This must be a nightmare. It had to be. But the doctor kept talking.

"A healthy kidney can be sold illegally for thousands of pounds," Dr Hussein was saying. "Anyway, I'll let you rest for a bit now. The police will be in later to ask questions." He paused. "Can you remember anything about what happened? Anything at all that you saw or heard?"

Curtis closed his eyes slowly. He tried, oh yes, he tried to remember. But all he could see was her long black hair, her dark hazel eyes and her dazzling smile.

And all he could hear was her talking softly into his ear: "I'm Pilar…"

THE END…

Dead Man Drinking

1

First day at work...

Jay woke to the shrill ringing of his reminder alarm. He reached out, turned it off and looked at the time. A quarter past six. Some sixteen-year-olds would have resented being woken up so early, but not Jay – not today. At the beginning of July, after what had seemed a lifetime, he had finally left school. Today was Jay's first day at work.

At seven, a battered builders' van pulled up outside Jay's house. He squeezed in the front, between the two characters who were going to become his workmates. There was Sam, who was a year or two older than Jay, and who had the letters "L", "U" and "V" tattooed on the knuckles of his right hand;

and Slug, who was in charge.

They had been hired to work on a large, rambling old house high up on the hill overlooking the town. The place was a total mess. Rainwater pipes were leaking, window frames were rotten, weeds were growing up through the drive and the paint on the front door was peeling.

"It's just been bought by some sort of scientist geezer, calls himself Professor," said Slug as they pulled up outside. "We've got to have this place ready for him to move into in a couple of months."

Slug set Jay to work pulling up the old drive with a heavy-duty breaker. It was hard going. After half an hour, Jay leant against an old tree for a bit of a rest. Suddenly, Slug appeared behind him.

"Right, kiddo," Slug said, "you're not at school now. You're being paid to work. Got it?"

Jay nodded.

"Do me a favour, though," Slug added, "fetch me a left-handed hammer from the van."

Jay didn't know what a left-handed hammer looked like, but he didn't want to look stupid, so he didn't say anything to Slug.

Jay searched through all the tools in the back of the van and tried to find something that looked like a left-handed hammer. A few minutes later, Slug and Sam walked round, laughing their heads off.

"Doh! There's no such thing as a left-handed hammer, is there?" chortled Sam. "It's a joke!"

Jay didn't think it was very funny.

~2~

He saw the word "RUM"...

The following day, during their lunch break, Jay was so tired he had a quick lie-down on a bench in the front garden. He woke up to the sound of Slug shouting at him:

"Get up! You lazy little—"

Jay stumbled to his feet and immediately fell flat on his face. Sam – or Slug – had tied his bootlaces together. Jay looked up and saw them both bent over with laughter.

Jay knew that he had to prove to them that he wasn't some sort of dopey kid. But how?

The answer came unexpectedly quickly

the next day. Jay was exploring the house and went down into the cellar. It was cold and damp. In the dim light of a single bulb dangling on a wire, Jay could see that it was empty, except for a large wooden barrel standing in the corner. Jay went over to inspect it. He saw the word "RUM" on the side.

Jay fetched a drill, a hammer and a piece of wood from the van. He drilled a hole in the side of the barrel, near the bottom and watched as the thick, golden liquid began to pour out. He plugged the hole with the piece of wood.

"Blimey, kiddo here is brighter than I thought," commented Slug as he put his finger in the small puddle of rum and licked it. He smiled and added, "You know, thanks to young Jay here, I think this could turn out to be a very sweet job indeed."

A strange bitter smell...

The next week, every lunchtime, and sometimes during tea break as well, they all went down to the cellar for a cup of rum. Jay was now definitely one of the lads. Things couldn't be better.

Next week, when Slug picked Jay up for work, he was on his own.

"Where's Sam?" asked Jay.

"Looks like he's done a runner," said Slug. "His mum hasn't seen him all weekend. She reckons he's got girlfriend trouble."

Jay frowned. They had last seen Sam on Friday afternoon. The Professor had turned up, paid them their wages and had measured up for furniture. Slug and Jay had driven off home, leaving Sam behind to finish off a bit of bricklaying. He'd seemed all right then.

Over the following days, Jay and Slug carried on drinking the rum. But without Sam it wasn't quite so much fun. Jay even thought the rum started to taste differently, more sour, with a strange bitter smell. He didn't say anything to Slug, though. He didn't want him to think he was a wimp.

Then, early Friday afternoon, Slug's phone rang.

"Yeah, Professor, I'm good. What can I do for you?" Jay heard Slug say. "Yeah... Right... No problem. Ten minutes, then." Slug finished the call, cursed and turned to Jay.

"The Professor wants us to take his barrel of rum out to the front drive. He needs it up the university."

Now it was Jay's turn to curse.

"He'll be here in ten with a van."

"He's bound to notice that we've been drinking it," said Jay.

"Course he is!" snapped Slug. "Well, come on. You got us into this mess. You got any ideas?"

Jay thought. "It's dead heavy that barrel, isn't it? So, supposing we accidentally drop it, getting it up the cellar steps? Then we say, 'Oops, sorry, Professor, we dropped the barrel and spilt a bit of your rum.'"

"Good idea!" said Slug, slapping his young workmate on the back. Jay felt a glow of pride. "Let's get down there and get started."

Down in the cellar, Jay and Slug grunted as they struggled to tilt and then roll the barrel to the bottom of the stone steps. Then they levered it up until they could heave it on to the third step.

"I reckon this will be high enough," Slug said. "Ready? Now!" And they both let go of the barrel. It clattered to the bottom of the steps, the wood cracking as it fell. When it hit the floor it splintered open along one side, spilling its contents. As the rum trickled out onto the stone cellar floor, the dank air was filled with a sickly sweet smell.

"Oops!" Slug said as they walked down the steps. Jay was about to say what a waste of great rum, but the words caught in his throat. He'd seen something sticking out of the barrel.

It was an arm – grey and puffy – but Jay could still see the letters "L", "U" and "V" tattooed on the sausage-sized fingers. The arm was severed at the elbow. White, shiny bone glistened in the dim light.

Slug saw the arm, too. Straightaway his knees buckled and he slumped heavily to the ground in a dead faint. Jay covered his

mouth and nose, but still he found himself retching violently. His vomit spewed down the steps and splattered on the floor. Jay turned quickly. He slipped on the sick and stumbled up the cellar steps. It was only when he was halfway up that he noticed a long, dark shadow had fallen across the steps in front of him. He looked up and saw a man standing over him.

"It seems you and your friend have been very careless. Very careless indeed, Jay," the Professor said, taking a step closer. "You see rum is very useful stuff. Before the days of chemicals and refrigeration and suchlike, it was used to preserve bodies. Dead bodies."

The dim light in the cellar caught in the Professor's hard, cruel eyes.

"You see, being a surgical pathologist – someone who studies the human body – I know about these things. That's why I need bodies – dead ones. And limbs, too, of course.

But you wouldn't believe just how difficult dead bodies and limbs are to get hold of these days." His face twisted into a chilling, deadly smile. "Still, your ex-friend Sam should keep me going for a bit. And then, after that, well…"

Jay saw the menacing glint of the surgeon's knife blade as the Professor pulled it from inside his jacket, and took another step down towards him and Slug. There was nowhere for him to run.

THE END…

DEADLY TALES

One book.
Two nightmares.

978 1 4451 0340 2 pb
978 1 4451 0855 1 eBook

978 1 4451 0337 2 pb
978 1 4451 0852 0 eBook

978 1 4451 0341 9 pb
978 1 4451 0856 8 eBook

978 1 4451 0336 5 pb
978 1 4451 0851 3 eBook

978 1 4451 0338 9 pb
978 1 4451 0853 7 eBook

Find out more about these books and
others published by EDGE at:
www.franklinwatts.co.uk

Plus visit Roy's website for the latest
news on all his books:
www.royapps.co.uk

DEADLY TALES
TEASER

Can't wait to find out what happens in the other DEADLY TALES urban legends? Well, here's a teaser from
The Party Animal

There were crisps and stuff, and I saw that Mia had put out the beef that Mum had put in the fridge for our sandwiches. There was hardly any left! I was grabbing the last slices, when I heard whimpering at the back door. Jasper, our pet dog had been shut outside! I bet no one at the snog-fest had even thought of feeding poor Jasper.

I opened the back door. I knew straight away that something was wrong. He seemed to be limping. I threw a few pieces of beef into his bowl. He staggered up to it, sicked up on the floor, then he toppled over wheezing like mad. What the…! I bent down to stroke his back, murmuring gently to him, while he groaned. Suddenly, his head lolled over onto the floor and he was completely still. Jasper! I shook him, but he was gone. Tears welled up in my eyes.

Slowly, a smile crept across my face. I knew what I had to do.

✝

Dare you to read the rest in:
DEADLY TALES
The Party Animal
and
Don't Look Under the Bed

Want to read more horror? Try iHorror by
The 2Steves, where you are the hero and
have to choose your own fate.

Fight your fear. Choose your fate.

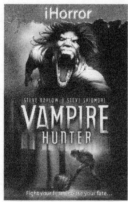

978 1 40830 985 8 pb
978 1 40831 476 0 eBook

978 1 40830 986 5 pb
978 1 40831 477 7 eBook

978 1 40830 988 9 pb
978 1 40831 479 1 eBook

978 1 40830 987 2 pb
978 1 40831 478 4 eBook

www.orchardbooks.co.uk